Busy Things That Go

By R. W. Alley

A GOLDEN BOOK • NEW YORK

Western Publishing Company, Inc., Racine, Wisconsin 53404

BRRRING, BRRRING!

"Hello," says Alex.

"Alex, what are you doing at home?" yells General Brown. "You are supposed to be here. You are going up today."

Alex looks at the alarm clock. "Oh, no," he gasps. "I forgot to wind it!"

Now Alex must really rush! He must travel past the plains, through the city, across the river, and over the mountains to reach the general. How will he ever get there in time?

Alex grabs his bag, hops on his scooter, and heads down the hill.

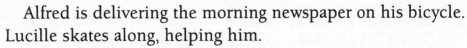

Alfred is delivering the morning newspaper on his bicycle. Lucille skates along, helping him.

"No time to look at the paper this morning," calls Alex.

"Good morning, Mr. Blinny," says Alex as he zips by.

Mr. Blinny's new sports car will not start. Tommy is coming with his tow truck to take the car to the garage. Mr. Blinny is not happy. He will have to drive his old station wagon to work.

Alex parks his scooter. It goes too slow to ride on the state road, so Alex must wait for the bus.

Cars stop to get gas. Cheryl checks the oil. Mike gets coffee for the grumpy carpool.

At last the bus comes. Alex hurries on.

There is a traffic jam on the state road. The signal light at the corner is broken. No one knows when to stop or go.

"Go! Go!" shouts Alex.

Walter is working on the problem from his electric company truck. From the cherry picker basket, he can reach the broken wire.

At the toll plaza everyone stops to pay. Cars pay a little bit. Alex's bus pays more. Big tractor trailers, like Thelma's, pay much more.

The Highway Department is building a new bridge in River Hollow.

The backhoe digs deep holes. The cement mixer pours in concrete to make the supports. Carefully Carlton picks up steel girders with his crane and lays them across the supports.

Bulldozers push up the surrounding ground to make a road. The grading machine smooths the slope, and the asphalt spreader pours down a layer of blacktop. Brian's steamroller comes last to smooth it flat and even.

Dennis and Darlene haul away the extra dirt in their dump truck. Many of the drivers on the highway slow down to watch the construction.

"Oh, hurry up, hurry up," Alex says. He's worried about being late.

At the village bus station all kinds of buses come and go. Mrs. Filbert drives a local bus. She takes workers to the offices and stores in the village. Shoppers ride the bus, too. There is also a big streamlined bus getting ready to leave the station. It will travel for many hours.

Alex dashes to the train depot. The train to the city is ready to leave the station.

"Hold the train!" calls Alex. He still has to buy a ticket.

Clyde, the conductor, waves on the train as Alex jumps aboard, taking a shortcut through the baggage car. Ethel, the engineer, checks the signal light to make sure there are no other trains on the track ahead. Then she opens the throttle.

TAILGATE
SPEEDWAY

WHOOO! WHOOO!
CLACKITY-CLACK!
The big diesel engine pulls the train cars along the steel track. Nearest the engine is the baggage car. It is filled with mail and luggage. Next is the sleeper car. It has small rooms with foldaway beds for passengers going on overnight trips. Day passengers relax in the coach car, which is next. In the café car the cook is trying to keep the soup from spilling. The last car is the observation car. Passengers sit in its glass dome to get a good view.

At the speedway mechanics and drivers are warming up their racing cars. There is a big race today. Sam tows his racing car behind his mobile home. "I'm too fast to live in one place," he says.

Even the hot dog stand is on wheels.

The train is stopping. The fence around a nearby cattle pasture is broken. There is a cow on the track. "Get off the track!" thinks Alex.

In the wide fields the farmer harvests his wheat with a combine machine. It separates the grain from the stalks and shoots it into the hopper wagon behind. Brenda pulls a plow with her tractor. She is turning the soil to get it ready to plant the next crop.

At the dairy barn fresh milk is pumped into a refrigerated tank truck. The tank will keep the milk cool all the way to the city.

Felix and Fergy drive a big-wheeled pickup truck over the rough and rocky sheep pasture.

In the hills a logging truck hauls newly cut timber out of the forest.

WHOOO! WHOOO!

The track is clear again.

CLACKITY-CLACK!

The train rolls on. "It's about time!" mutters Alex.

Just outside the city the train tracks branch off in all directions. One branch goes to the auto plant. There, new automobiles are loaded onto special railroad cars.

Another branch of the track leads to the truck depot. Rollie hooks up his truck tractor to a trailer and drives it right off the railroad car.

In the shops diesel and steam engines are repaired.

Sondra in the signal tower must keep it all straight. She throws the switches that make the trains go this way or that. WHOOO! WHOOO!

Ethel, the engineer, pulls the whistle to say hello to Cole, the engineer on a train that has just brought the circus to the city.

Alex looks at his watch. "I guess I don't have time to watch the circus unload," he thinks.

Everyone rushes at Main Street Station. Commuters hurry on and off local trains. Vacationers carry lots of luggage onto the express trains. Some trains even let passengers take their automobiles with them.

Paul the postal worker unloads bags of mail onto Stella's electric truck. Stella zips the mail through the station to the post office next door. After the letters and packages are sorted, trucks and vans will deliver them all through the city.

Alex hurries down the stairs into the subway. Subway trains run in underground tunnels below the city's streets and buildings. They carry people all over the city.

WHOOOOSH!

The trains come speeding into the subway station and stop.

BONG! BONG!

Dan, the conductor, makes sure everyone is inside the subway cars before he goes.

After Alex leaves the subway, he finds a taxi cab.
"Where to, sir?" asks Conrad, the cabdriver.
"To the docks, and please hurry!" says Alex.
"You're in luck! I know a shortcut!" the cabbie cries.
HONK! HONK!
Conrad dodges in and out between stopped vans and long limousines.
"Hold on! Big pothole ahead," calls Conrad.
THUMP!
"This is worse than a roller coaster!" thinks Alex.
Everything is crowded on the city streets. The buses need two levels to fit all the people who want to ride.

OOPS!

Conrad slams on his brakes. The insurance company is on fire. The police cars block traffic so the fire trucks can get through.

Chief Kathy directs her fire fighters. The ladder truck reaches up high. The pumper truck shoots water from the hydrants on the street out through the hoses.

Dr. Florence waits with her ambulance just in case someone is hurt.

Cleo, on the TV news truck, takes pictures of it all.

"Oh, my, I don't have time for all this!" says Alex.

DING! DING!

Alex hops on the trolley. It rattles on its narrow tracks down the hill to the docks.

TOOT! TOOT!

All day long Francine's ferry carries people, cars, and trucks back and forth across the choppy harbor. Alex leaps on, just in time!

Up the river a big tug tows a string of barges. Other tugs push an oil tanker to a special dock.

"Be careful with that hook!" calls out Larry, a longshoreman. A crane on wheels unloads the heaviest cargo from a big freighter. Smaller cranes built right on the ship's deck swing lighter crates onto the dock.

In the middle of all the big ships a fleet of fishing boats is returning with the day's catch.

"Ahoy!" calls Captain Smith. "How about some halibut?"

The lightship shows other ships the entrance to the harbor. The lightship's commander must make sure his ship doesn't drift.

The great ocean liner *Smedley* is steaming back from a cruise.

WHAAA! WHAAA!

A fireboat blows its horn and sprays fountains of water to greet her.

SPLASH!

A big anchor is dropped from an aircraft carrier. It has a deck with a landing strip. Pilots in small planes take off from the carrier. They will make short flights and then practice landing on the carrier's deck.

Tom sprays by in his Hovercraft. The Hovercraft glides over the water.

"I wish this ferry were that fast," says Alex, checking his watch.

Commodore Neville's submarine travels underwater.

On the other side of the river sailboats catch the wind and race each other around the harbor buoys. There's quite a crowd watching from the old riverboat *Queenie*. Sergeant Quig watches from his police speedboat, making sure no one gets in the way of the race.

At Brightbeach Yacht Club the *Bay Breeze* ties up. It is called a tall ship because it has high masts that carry its sails.

Flynn rents his powerboat for fishing trips on the ocean.
Helen fishes right from her houseboat. "What's your rush?"
she calls to Alex.
"I have to get over the mountains!"
"Try the balloons!" suggests Helen. She points toward
the park.

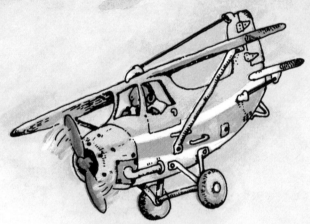

"Never fear!" cries Alvin. "My balloon will get you over the mountains in no time!"

Alvin unties the ropes, tosses out the sandbags, and the balloon floats up and up. It is cold high in the sky over the mountaintops.

Hikers are walking up the mountain, carrying packs on their backs. They will camp in the mountains. Higher up, climbers scale the steep face of the mountain. They use ropes and hooks to attach themselves to a rock.

WHOOSH!

A big jet airliner zooms by above.

WHIRRR-WHIRRR-WHIRRR!

A small private plane passes below.

"We must be near the airport," says Alvin.

BAGGAGE

Chris, the controller, tells the airplanes when and where to take off and land. Flight 37 is just landing. The pilot lowers the landing gear so his jet can land safely. At the same moment Flight 1010 takes off. Propeller engines whir as they pull the plane through the air.

Passengers are lining up at Gate 5 for another flight. It looks like they are going somewhere warm. Bob brings the baggage train around to load the luggage. Margo drives the food truck. Fawn drives the fuel truck.

Alex jumps out of the balloon's basket. "Oh, dear. I only have a few minutes. How will I ever make it there in time?"

"Where are you going?" shouts Hank. Hank has a helicopter.

GATE 5

FINE FLYING FOODS INC.

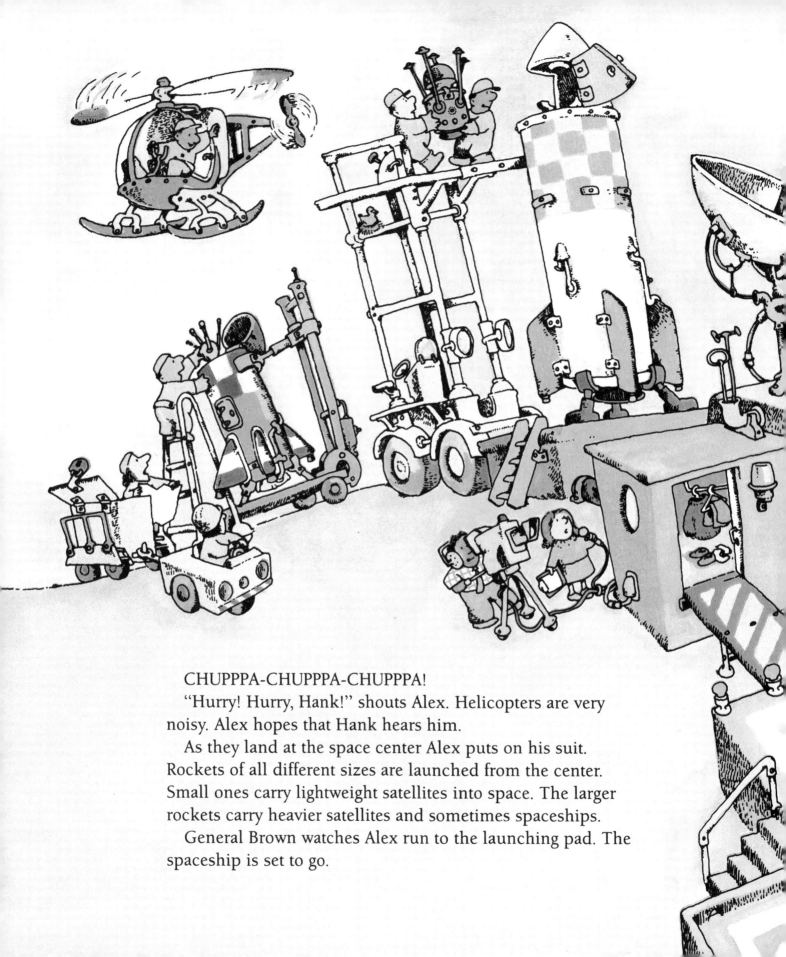

CHUPPPA-CHUPPPA-CHUPPPA!

"Hurry! Hurry, Hank!" shouts Alex. Helicopters are very noisy. Alex hopes that Hank hears him.

As they land at the space center Alex puts on his suit. Rockets of all different sizes are launched from the center. Small ones carry lightweight satellites into space. The larger rockets carry heavier satellites and sometimes spaceships.

General Brown watches Alex run to the launching pad. The spaceship is set to go.

"T-minus 60 seconds!" General Brown calls over the loudspeaker. He has begun the countdown.

"T-minus 30 seconds!"

The blast-off will take place soon. The space center workers are taking cover.

"T-minus 15 seconds!"

Alex races up the tower.

"T-minus 5 seconds!"

The tower moves away from the rocket.

"T-minus 4, 3, 2, 1, BLAST-OFF!

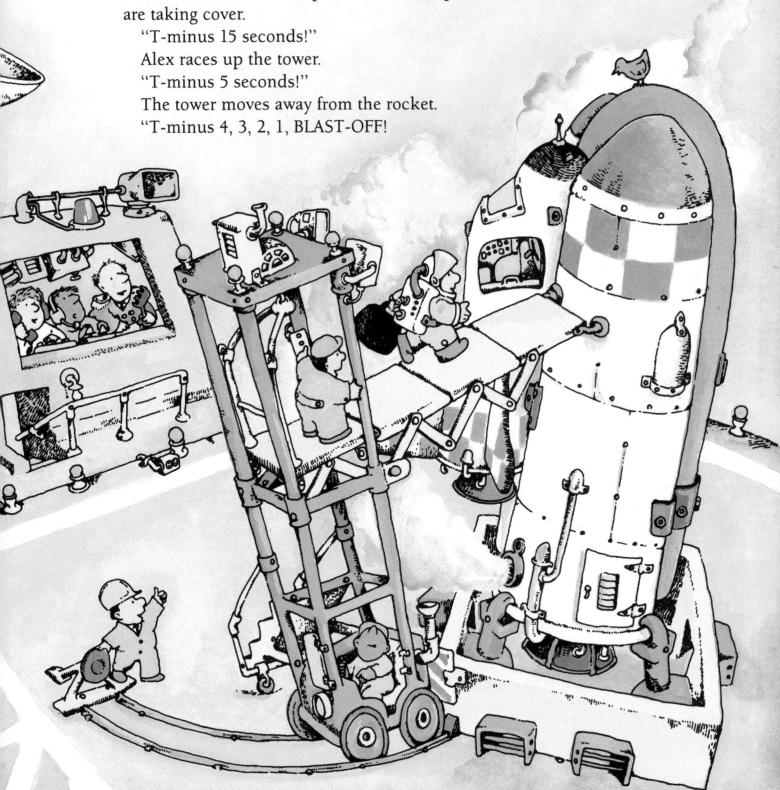

"Happy trip, Alex," radios General Brown.

Astronaut Alex has made it! In seconds his spaceship takes him up through the blue sky into black, black space.

Once the rocket's fuel is burned up, it falls back to Earth. Alex keeps going in the orbiter. He is bringing supplies to astronauts building a space station.

Alex must be careful not to bump into any of the many satellites going around Earth. There are other spaceships, too. One lands on the moon. Another is getting ready to go to Mars. It will travel for a year to get there. But there is one spaceship Alex does not recognize.

"I wonder where that one is from!" he thinks.